MILO'S CHRISTMAS PARADE

The artwork for this book was made using pencil, ink, watercolor, and digital tools.

Cataloging-in-Publication Data has been applied for and may be obtained from the Library of Congress.

ISBN 978-1-4197-4499-0

Printed and bound in China
10 9 8 7 6 5 4 3 2 1

Abrams Books for Young Readers are available at special discounts when purchased in quantity for premiums and promotions as well as fundraising or educational use. Special editions can also be created to specification. For details, contact specialsales@abramsbooks.com or the address below.

Abrams® is a registered trademark of Harry N. Abrams, Inc.

ABRAMS The Art of Books
195 Broadway, New York, NY 10007
abramsbooks.com

MILO'S
CHRISTMAS
PARADE

Jennie Palmer

Abrams Books for Young Readers • New York

Milo's family never missed the big Christmas parade.
His passel came for the popcorn, sticky nuts, and bits of peppermint sticks.

Milo came for the view.

The parade was always over too soon for Milo.
Luckily, he knew where to find it.

The other opossums had no interest in
the busy building near their home.

But inside the building was Milo's favorite place.
Everything for the parade was made there, and
it was Christmas all year long.

He loved things like this,*

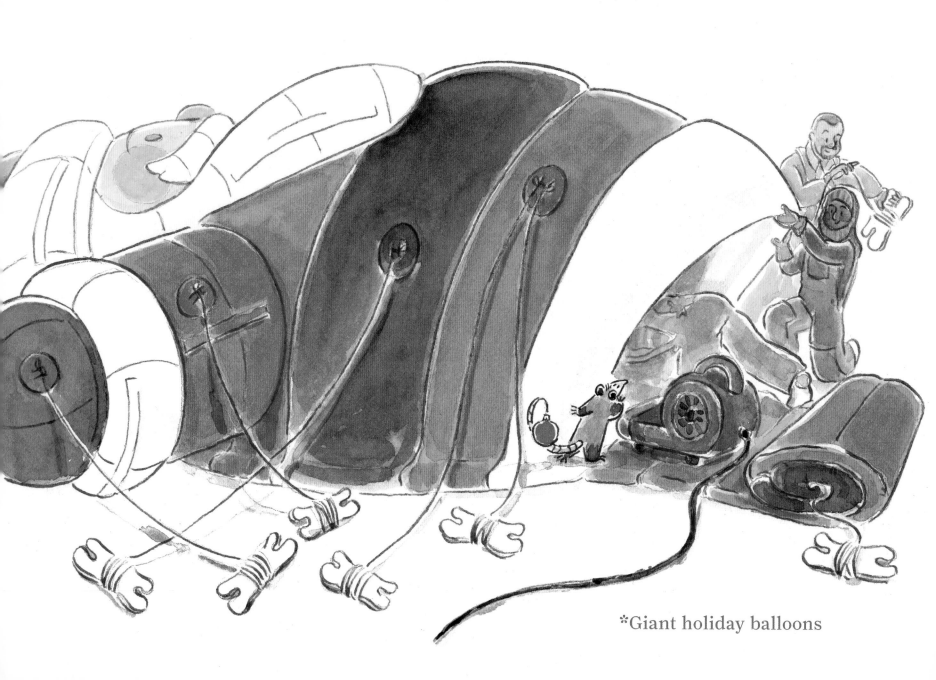

*Giant holiday balloons

and this,*

*Painted poinsettias

and whatever this stuff* was.

*Float fringe!

1962

1982

2003

These were not opossum things, but he didn't care.
Being in the Christmas parade was Milo's dream.

Every year Milo hoped his dream
would come true.

It never did.

This year, he decided, would be different.

Milo would take matters into his own paws.

But he couldn't do it alone.

Milo needed his family's help.

And though they didn't understand his dream, opossums stick together.

Some jobs they took to immediately.

Milo handled the rest.*

*Float bed construction

*Paint

*Trim

*Fringe!

He worked steadily throughout the year.
Until every detail was just so.

Parade day came.
Milo thought his float looked fantastic.
He could not wait to show it off.

The opossums squeezed into the lineup,
but they parked in the path of a giant balloon . . .

The passel scattered in the nick of time.

Milo watched his dream come crashing down.

Not everyone was ready to give up.
His family didn't understand Milo's dream,
but they believed in him.

While Milo made repairs,
his passel made sure he was
not disturbed.*

Ew.

*Opossums play dead.

By the time he was finished,
the tail end of the parade was small in the distance.

Milo was not discouraged.
His new float was sturdy and sleek.
It rocketed down the road on pure passel power.

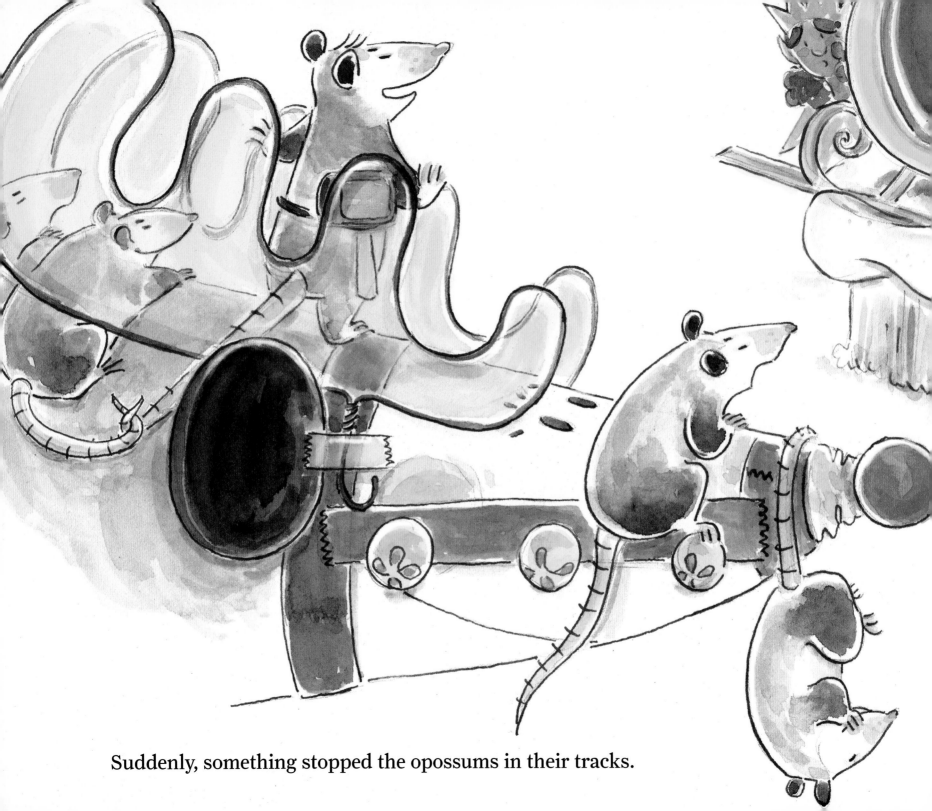

Suddenly, something stopped the opossums in their tracks.

Despite his float's predicament, Santa was calm, as if he had been expecting Milo all along.

Milo was starstruck.

He offered assistance, which was graciously accepted.

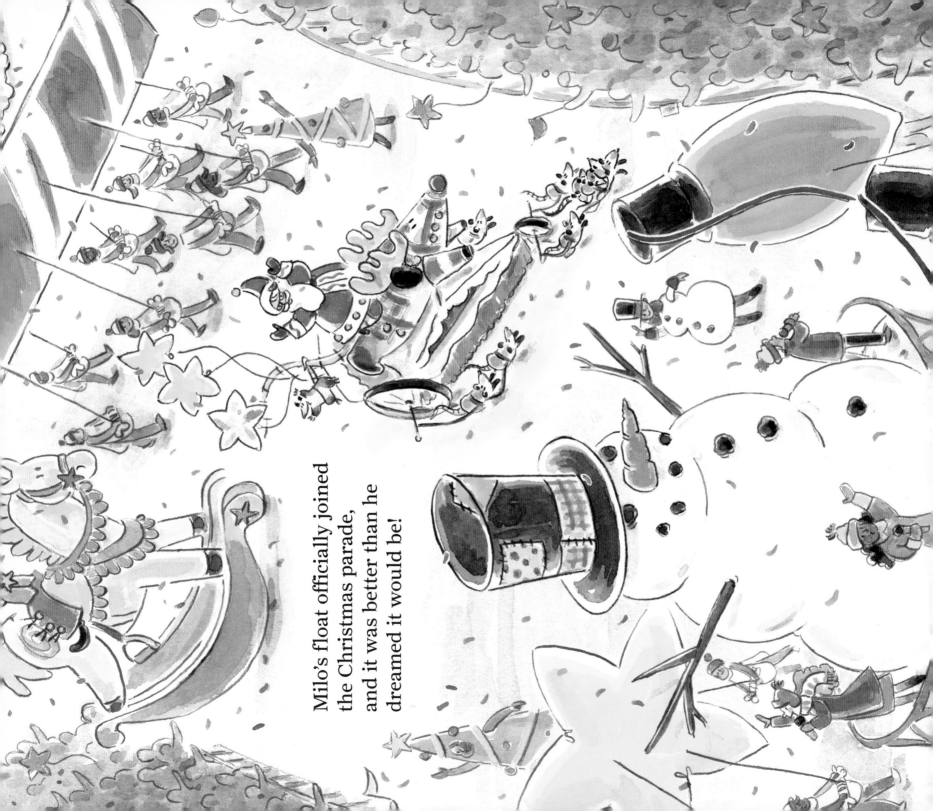

Milo's float officially joined the Christmas parade, and it was better than he dreamed it would be!

The parade crew admired Milo's float.
It was rough around the edges but built from the heart.

"I think," said the crew leader,
"we have just the place for an opossum like you."

And that was how Milo joined the Christmas parade.*

*With the help of a passel who believed in him.

Because nothing should keep an opossum from their dream.

AUTHOR'S NOTE

In the fourth grade, I made a giant paper hot dog in art class. I remember folding the outside ends of the large sheet of craft paper to meet in the center and stuffing the sides with crumpled scraps, until it miraculously resembled a bun. That experience changed me, and I have been chasing that paper-hot dog feeling ever since. I built theater sets, props, and puppets before finally landing at Macy's, designing and building floats and balloons for their Thanksgiving Day Parade.

In the time I worked at Macy's, we created giant turtles and Egyptian tombs, space stations and cherry pies. Each float is built like a puzzle. They fold up to fit through tight tunnels and snake down narrow city streets, only to be reassembled early Thanksgiving morning. The job was my fourth-grade dream come true.

At the parade studio, I worked with many talented designers, engineers, carpenters, welders, painters, electricians, sculptors, and balloonatics. They were my passel, and there is a bit of each of them in Milo's scrappy spirit. This book is dedicated to the Macy's studio crew, for the work they do all year long to prepare for one epic three-hour celebration. It is a privilege to make something that brings joy to so many people, and I cannot think of a better dream to have—for a person or an opossum.